**www.raintreepublishers.co.uk**
Visit our website to find out
more information about
Raintree books.

**To order:**
☎ Phone 0845 6044371
📄 Fax +44 (0) 1865 312263
📧 Email myorders@raintreepublishers.co.uk

Customers from outside the UK please telephone +44 1865 312262

Raintree is an imprint of Capstone Global Library Limited,
a company incorporated in England and Wales having its
registered office at 7 Pilgrim Street, London, EC4V 6LB
– Registered company number: 6695582

First published by Stone Arch Books in 2011
First published in the United Kingdom in 2012
The moral rights of the proprietor have been asserted.

Art Director: Bob Lentz
Designer: Brann Garvey
Production Specialist: Michelle Biedschied
Editor: Vaarunika Dharmapala
Originated by Capstone Global Library Ltd
Printed and bound in China by Leo Paper Products Ltd

ISBN 978 1 406 22715 4 (paperback)
15 14 13 12 11
10 9 8 7 6 5 4 3 2

**British Library Cataloguing in Publication Data**
A full catalogue record for this book is available
from the British Library.

# CONTENTS

# CHAPTER 1

# MEGA-ERUPTION

Barry Allen frowned as he watched
the evening news. The scene on the screen
was beautiful, showing a brilliant tropical
landscape. The Pacific Ocean sparkled
in the sunlight, and waves lapped at the
golden sands.

Mount Lavalo, the biggest mountain
on the island of Wiji, stood tall against a
clear blue sky. It was lovely to look at. But
Barry, who was secretly the Flash, was not
concerned with how Mount Lavalo looked.
He was concerned with how it was acting.

"A number of recent earthquakes in the South Pacific have scientists worried," said the reporter on the television. "According to geologists, a mega-eruption on Mount Lavalo is coming soon. Although dormant for 83 years, strong evidence suggests that this could be the biggest and most lethal eruption Wiji has ever seen."

Barry groaned. He knew that these mega-eruptions could destroy half a continent with their boiling lava. Their ash could also block the Sun for months.

"Homes and businesses are being evacuated," the reporter continued. "But, if the predictions are true, no amount of preparation can help this doomed nation."

The screen flashed to several historic volcanic eruptions. In each case, the skies were blackened by tonnes of grey ash.

None of these historic eruptions were mega-eruptions. Human beings had never witnessed one before – this would be the first in 30,000 years.

As the Flash, Barry Allen was blindingly fast and capable of incredible feats. When it came to a mega-eruption, though, the Flash was in over his head. He could do a lot of things, but he could not prevent the biggest volcanic eruption in history – not by himself, anyway.

"The only way to stop the eruption is to cool the magma chamber," a scientist on the television told the reporter. "But that's impossible. It would require an enormous amount of refrigeration in order to lower the temperature of the super-heated heart of the volcano."

"Impossible?" Barry repeated.

The World's Fastest Man was sure that cooling this pool of molten rock beneath this volcano was possible. In fact, he knew one person who could handle the task.

"But *would* he?" Barry said aloud. He did not like the idea that was creeping into his brain. How could he team up with his arch-enemy? How could he join forces with a super-villain?

"This island could disappear under a heap of molten lava forever," said the television reporter.

Barry Allen sighed. An entire nation was in grave danger, and he could think of only one way to help. "I have no choice."

Captain Cold had recently been released from prison. The conditions of his parole were strict.

He had to make his location known to police at all times. Barry was a police scientist, so finding the criminal's mobile phone number was not hard.

"I'm busy!" Captain Cold shouted into the phone. "What do you want?"

On the other end of the line, Flash closed his eyes and gritted his teeth. This was the last thing he wanted to say. "Your help," he admitted quietly.

**HAHAHAHA!** Captain Cold laughed like an Arctic wolf. "Oh, Flash, you puny little speedster," he said. "I just knew you'd come calling one day. But what makes you desperate enough to ask for my help?"

"A volcano," Flash explained, trying to keep himself cool. "The biggest eruption the world has ever seen."

Flash knew that Captain Cold would not care about the volcano, the island it would destroy, or the people who would die. Cold was a criminal mastermind who left a trail of destruction behind him wherever he went. But his ego was huge. He was sure to care about the attention he would get for stopping the biggest eruption in history. The challenge would be hard to refuse.

"The biggest?" Captain Cold asked.

Flash could hear the interest in his voice. "Yes," the super hero confirmed. "The biggest. And I need your help to stop it."

Captain Cold was silent for a moment. "Come to my laboratory, and we'll talk," he said. "But make it quick, or I just might change my mind."

Barry Allen hung up the phone and pressed the gold ring on his finger.

# KLIKKK!

A tiny square of folded fabric shot out from inside the high-tech jewellery. As soon as it hit the air, the fabric began to expand. Seconds later, it was a life-sized uniform. The super hero slipped inside at super-speed, and his transformation was complete.

# CHAPTER 2

# CUTTING A DEAL

The Flash raced through Central City, a crimson streak of light against the dark night. Citizens heard the quiet roar as he sped by. They felt a warm breeze from his lightning-fast vibrations. But all they saw was a blazing trail of red and gold.

The Flash zoomed past blocks of flats, department stores, corner shops, and petrol stations. He sped past them all, making his way towards the abandoned buildings on the edge of the river.

On the far side of a string of rundown warehouses, Flash screeched to a halt in front of a large, steel door.

The steel doors opened. "I hope this isn't a mistake," the Flash said to himself as he entered the villain's lab.

In the dark shadows, the Flash could just about make out the shape of Captain Cold's hood and the barrel of his weapon. The super-crook was pointing his freeze gun right at him!

"*Move!*" said a voice in Flash's head. But the super hero remained still. Showing fear would only give Captain Cold the upper hand in their temporary partnership.

"Freeze!" Captain Cold said, laughing.

"Very funny," replied the Flash.

Captain Cold dropped the weapon to his side. "I thought so," he agreed. He held the door open wide and smiled wickedly. "That was quick, even for you."

Flash stepped further inside, ready to spring into super-speed at any second. He had never been to this hideout before. Caution was always wise in a new setting, especially when Captain Cold was near by.

Dirty light bulbs on the ceiling lit up the warehouse laboratory. The Flash's eyes widened when he saw a collection of giant freeze guns on a nearby table.

"You're not the only one who follows the news, Flash," Captain Cold said. "I know all about the eruption of Mount Lavalo. But you're forgetting something – I'm not in the business of stopping disasters."

The Flash knew that Captain Cold would not stop the eruption because it was the right thing to do. The chance to face his greatest challenge might not be enough motivation, either. The villain would need a stronger reason, such as fame or fortune.

"The island of Wiji would be forever in your debt," the Flash began. "They might even offer a handsome reward."

Captain Cold's eyes gleamed behind his radio-receiver glasses. "Do I have your word that you'll help me get the credit I deserve?" he asked.

"You have my word," the Flash said.

"You're such a goody-goody," said Captain Cold. "The task isn't difficult, really – at least not for a brilliant mastermind like me."

The Flash ignored Captain Cold's words. He looked past the villain to the machinery and freeze guns sitting on the table.

"Impressive, aren't they?" the villain said. "It just so happens that your timing is excellent. I've been working on some new technology that has even more freezing power! Your little eruption gives me the perfect opportunity to test it out."

"It's not my eruption, Cold," the Flash corrected. "It's Mother Nature's."

Captain Cold packed several freeze guns into a special, weather-proof bag. "Mother Nature has nothing on Old Man Winter," he said with a laugh.

HAHAHAHA!

# CHAPTER 3

# EARTHQUAKE!

**BZZT!** A few hours later, Captain Cold stood on top of the giant volcano, firing a freeze gun down into its throat. With his special glasses, the super-villain could see deep into the crater, but not as far as the magma chamber. Every minute or two, when Cold felt another powerful blast, he fired again. **BZZT!**

"I could help if you'd lend me a cold gun," the Flash said. He was not eager to use one of the weapons. As a rule, the Flash was weapon-free.

But the speedy super hero felt foolish just standing around doing nothing.

"Are you sure you could handle it?" Captain Cold began to say.

**RUMMMMMMMBLE!** Suddenly, Mount Lavalo began to shake. It rocked slowly at first and then shuddered violently.

"Earthquake!" shouted Flash.

**CRAAAAACK!** A gaping hole opened up in the ground near by. Trees were uprooted and crashed to the ground. A giant boulder broke free and started to roll down the mountain. The Flash whirled into action, racing down the steep, rocky slope. **WHOOOOSH!**

Not far below, the Flash could see a group of people scrambling for cover on the path.

One of them was carrying a television camera. *Probably a crew on their way up to document the volcano,* Flash thought. He sped up and leapt over the boulder easily, but he still had to stop it. The massive rock was heading straight at the crew.

"Look out below!" the Scarlet Speedster warned. They could not hear him over the roar of the earthquake.

## THUD! THUD! THUD!

The giant rock thundered down the mountain.  It crashed into a fallen tree, crunched through part of the trunk, and kept on going.

Flash moved so fast he was nothing but a blur, racing further and further in front of the rock. Then suddenly, he turned around and headed straight at it.

Moving faster than the speed of light, he vibrated right into the centre of the tumbling boulder. He spun dizzily for a moment, and then he began to pulsate with all his strength.

**KA-POW!** The giant rock shattered into a thousand pieces. Several chunks landed at the feet of the reporters, who stared at the Flash in shock.

"Thank you!" the man holding the camera said as the ground became still.

"No problem," the Flash said.

Meanwhile, Captain Cold kept firing his cold gun into the volcano. The villain mopped his brow. "It's way too hot up here!" he shouted. "If I'd have known how much heat I'd have to take stopping this thing, I would've stayed at home!"

The ground had stopped rumbling, and Captain Cold looked around at the tropical island. From the top of Mount Lavalo he could see almost everything – sparkling sea, sandy beaches, and green trees. It was pretty, he had to admit, but it was also hot. And Captain Cold hated the heat.

Captain Cold untied his hood and pulled it off. A light breeze ruffled his dark hair. *That's better,* he thought.

The villain felt a bead of sweat snake down his back. "I hate hot!" he shouted. "I despise tropical!" He fired the cold gun at the left side of the summit. *BZZT!*

Instantly, a whole patch of tropical island was frozen solid. *BZZT!* He fired the gun on the right, creating another frosty patch. Ice spread out in front of him. *BZZT! BZZT! BZZT!*

A slow smile spread across his face as he pulled his hood back up. He looked around and laughed crazily.

Captain Cold had a new plan.

# CHAPTER 4

# COLD SNAP!

At the base of the volcano, Flash felt a strange chill and looked around, confused. The average temperature on the island was 30 degrees Celsius. So why did he just shiver?

Looking up, he shivered again. This time it was not the air that chilled him. It was the sight of frozen palm trees. Entire sections of the top of Mount Lavalo were frozen solid with ice!

"That dirty crook!" Flash said under his breath. "Captain Cold's up to no good."

"What did you say?" one of the nearby reporters asked.

The Scarlet Speedster's face turned as red as his uniform. "Um, nothing," he replied. "I have to go!" He sped up the mountain like a race car.

"I should have known Captain Cold couldn't be trusted!" the Flash scolded himself. "It was stupid to leave him alone up there!"

The higher the Flash climbed, the cooler the air became. Luckily, the super hero's vibrations created their own heat and kept him from getting cold. The ground was slippery in places. Snow and ice slowed him down. He had to be very careful not to slip and fall.

When he reached the summit, Flash saw Captain Cold firing his freeze gun at everything in sight.

"What are you doing?" the Flash shouted.

"What does it look like?" Captain Cold replied. "I'm cooling the place off. You said I had to stop the eruption. Well, I'm stopping it. And while I'm at it, I thought I'd give this island a much needed cold snap." The villain threw his head back and laughed. "I always wanted my own personal tundra!"

Captain Cold pointed his freeze gun at a hibiscus tree covered in beautiful pink blossoms and fired. **BZZT!** A second later, the entire plant was frozen. The flowers fell to the icy ground and shattered.

"You won't get any gratitude from the island residents if you destroy their beautiful nation!" the Flash said. "They'll hate you!"

**HAHAHAHA!** Captain Cold roared. "You just don't get it, do you, Flash?" he said. "Why would I give a hoot about their petty little gratitude when I can claim my own frozen island?"

Flash felt foolish for trying to reason with the icy evil-doer. How many times would he make that mistake? *Probably a hundred,* the super hero admitted to himself. The Flash always looked for the best in others – always wanted to give them the chance to show that they had some good inside.

*Forget it,* Flash told himself.

Whirling into action, Flash placed himself between Captain Cold and the section of jungle he was aiming at.

**BZZZT!** Captain Cold fired, and the Flash roared through the stream of ice. His vibrations were so fast that they created intense heat and melted the ice.

Captain Cold's face wrenched into a ball of fury. "You can't stop me!" he shrieked. "You don't have the power to stop me!"

The villain turned and fired again, but the Flash was ready.

**VROOOOOM!** He sped right into the stream of ice, melting it again.

"Arrgghh!" Captain Cold bellowed. He turned to fire in another direction, but the same thing happened. He would never get his own personal tundra at this rate!

Captain Cold cracked a wicked smile. He aimed his freeze gun again. Only this time, he lowered the muzzle and fired at the ground beneath Flash's feet.

**WHAM!** Flash slipped and fell hard on to the ice.

"Oh, did that hurt?" Captain Cold said with a laugh. He raised his gun again and fired. **BZZZT!**

Flash tried to get up. The icy ground was so slippery he was running on the spot.

Captain Cold fired in every direction, aiming further down the mountain. Flash saw the television crew in the distance, completely frozen.

He had to do something ... and fast.

So Flash ran. His boots moved up and down like pistons. After a minute, the ice under his feet began to melt. Soon he was standing in a puddle. Luckily, Captain Cold was having such a good time freezing everything in sight he did not notice that Flash had melted the ice slick that had kept him running on the spot. The super hero had the advantage.

In an instant, the Flash became a streak of red. He raced in circles around Mount Lavalo, starting at the top and working his way down. He used all his superhuman strength to move as fast as he could. He left a path of vibrating warmth behind him, liquefying the snow wherever he went. Captain Cold's frozen island was suddenly having a warm spring day.

"You boy scout!" Captain Cold shouted. He tightened his grip on his freeze gun. "You're no match for me!"

The villain ran to the area where he was storing his weapons and dashed inside. When Captain Cold reappeared, he was carrying the biggest, most powerful freeze gun the world had ever seen. **ZZZAPPPPPP!** He fired it down the side of Mount Lavalo, covering an entire square kilometre with solid ice.

"Take that!" he shouted.

Flash nearly fell on a newly formed patch of ice, but he managed to remain upright. The super hero screeched to a halt and looked around, grimly. With his new freeze gun, Captain Cold was even more powerful than before.

Being fast would not be enough to stop Captain Cold's spreading trail of ice. The Flash was starting to run out of ideas.

# CHAPTER 5

# SHOWDOWN

The giant freeze gun was firing so fast that Flash's head spun just watching the ice form. Furious, he charged at the evil-doer. "That's enough!" the Flash shouted.

"I'm just getting started!" Captain Cold replied. He aimed the freeze gun at Flash.

The Fastest Man Alive darted aside so quickly that Captain Cold did not see where he went. Guessing, he turned to his right and fired again.

A bubble of hot air came out of the top of the volcano like a burp. Flash raced up to the summit and peered into the throat. He was greeted by another gush of gas.

"Enough of this!" the Flash called to Captain Cold. "Hand me a gun! The chamber is heating up again. We need to cool it down, or we'll both die!"

ZZZAPPPPPP! Captain Cold fired in a giant circle as he huffed his way up the volcano. "I'll handle it," the villain said, reaching the summit.

Captain Cold peered into the super-hot crater and was met by another steamy burst. He fired down the volcano's throat, watching it freeze. "You see how easy it is to tame Mother Nature?" he boasted. "I'm a hundred times more powerful than she is!"

He fired into the air, and icy pellets rained down on the volcano. "A *thousand times* more powerful!"

Flash watched Captain Cold refreeze the areas he had just thawed. The super hero began to understand just how crazy the villain had become. *I was foolish to think he would co-operate,* Flash thought.

"The volcano is going to erupt!" the Flash yelled. "Your job is to stop it."

"I'd rather stop you!" Captain Cold replied.

The villain aimed his weapon at Flash again. But this time, instead of dodging the blast of ice, Flash faced it head on. He stared down the barrel of the ice gun. He concentrated hard.

Like a volcano building up pressure beneath the surface, Flash boosted the energy inside himself. The super hero recharged himself with speed until he was about to explode.

*Captain Cold won't see this coming,* he thought. Then, Flash erupted, blasting at the villain's Freeze Ray. Moving too fast to be seen, the Scarlet Speedster disabled the weapon before the villain could even notice.

Captain Cold pulled the trigger. Nothing happened.

**CLICK! CLICK!** Captain Cold pulled the trigger over and over. Nothing.

"What have you done?" Captain Cold screamed.

"Nothing much," the Flash said.

The super hero smiled and moved slowly towards the villain. Flash knew the weapon could not be used against him anymore.

**CLICK! CLICK!** Captain Cold tried again, but the gun would not fire.

In a rage, Captain Cold threw the useless gun aside and tackled Flash. The super hero was so surprised it took him a second to realize what had happened – just enough time for Captain Cold to wrestle him to the ground.

Unfortunately for Captain Cold, the Flash did not just run with blinding speed. He wrestled with blinding speed, too. In less than two seconds, Captain Cold was pinned down.

Flash reached for the freeze gun the criminal mastermind had thrown aside.

"Ooof!" Captain Cold elbowed the Flash in the side and tried to grab the gun.

**BZZT!** The gun accidentally fired, freezing Captain Cold!

"Your own personal tundra," the Flash said with a chuckle. "Looks like you got what you wanted after all." He thought he heard a squeaky sound come from the frozen figure.

"Don't worry," Flash told him. "You'll only be frozen long enough for me to get this volcano under control."

Flash carried the mega-freeze gun to the crater and fired several times down its throat. The rumbling in the volcano's belly stopped. The magma was cooling down.

All at once, Flash knew what to do.

The super hero collected several freeze guns and carefully put them in one of Captain Cold's bags. Then he sped down the volcano to the nearest science station. He handed the guns – and a quickly-written note explaining Captain Cold's plan – to the head geologist. He explained that these specially developed weapons could help stop the mega-eruption. Moments later, he was back at the top of Mount Lavalo.

"And now for you," the Flash said. He picked up the frozen shape that was Captain Cold and carried him to a recently formed lava lake, which was still partly churning and bubbling.

He deposited the villain right next to the hot lava and stood back to watch him thaw.

"I told you I wouldn't make you stay frozen for long," he chuckled. "Maybe now you'll chill out a little!"

*     *     *

Barry Allen smiled as he looked at the television screen. It showed a warm, tropical landscape. The Pacific Ocean sparkled in the Sun. Waves lapped on golden sands. Mount Lavalo, the biggest mountain on Wiji, stood tall against a clear blue sky. It was lovely to look at. And thanks to the Flash, Mount Lavalo was no longer a threat.

"Scientists are reporting that thanks to an amazing new technology in the form of an ice gun, they are able to control the temperature of the magma chamber deep in the heart of Mount Lavalo," said the reporter.

"The threat of a mega-eruption has been snuffed out," the reporter said, smiling.

"In other news," continued the reporter, "the Flash alerted authorities to a man in a strange hooded outfit near the base of Mount Lavalo. The police recognized him as the criminal mastermind Captain Cold. The super-villain was quickly arrested for leaving his home state, a violation of his parole."

Barry knew that Captain Cold would be cooling off for a long while ... in prison.

CAPTAIN COLD

# CAPTAIN COLD

**REAL NAME: LEONARD SNART**

**OCCUPATION: PROFESSIONAL CRIMINAL**

**HEIGHT: 1.87 METRES**

**WEIGHT: 89 KILOGRAMS**

**EYES: BROWN**

**HAIR: BROWN**

**SPECIAL POWERS/ABILITIES:**

Wields a cold gun that can lower any object's temperature to absolute zero; his nerves of ice and his cold heart let him remain cool and collected even when the heat is on; he's also a skilled marksman.

done

● ○ ○                    CAPTAIN COLD BIO

◀ ▶ ⟳ ● 🏠 [                                    ]    [            🔍]

## BIOGRAPHY:

Leonard Snart once terrorized Central City with a spree
of cold-hearted crimes. No one could escape Captain
Cold's icy grip – until the Flash turned up and put the
super-villain on ice! Snart knew that if he wanted to stay
out of jail, he would have to find a way to combat his
super-speedy rival. So, he created an ultra-cold cannon
that is capable of bringing even the Scarlet Speedster to
a standstill! With the tide turned, Captain Cold looks to
use this advantage to stop the Flash in his tracks.

CAPTAIN COLD EXTRAS

[                                    ]    [            🔍]

S:

Snart's snow goggles prevent him from being
blinded by the ultra-bright flash of his cold guns.

The snow parka Snart wears keeps the cold out,
protecting him from even sub-zero temperatures.

Captain Cold has ice grenades that can freeze
everything in sight. Approach him with caution.

# BIOGRAPHIES

**Jane Mason** is no super hero, but having three kids sometimes makes her wish she had superpowers. Jane has written children's books for more than fifteen years and hopes to continue doing so for fifty more. She lives with her husband, three children, their dog, and a gecko.

From an early age, **Dan Schoening** has had a passion for animation and comic books. Dan currently does freelance work in the animation and games industries and spends a lot of time with his lovely little daughter, Paige.

**Mike DeCarlo** is a long-term contributor of comic art whose range extends from Batman and Iron Man to Bugs Bunny and Scooby-Doo. He lives with his wife and four children.

**Lee Loughridge** has been working in comics for more than fifteen years. He currently lives in a tent on the beach.

# GLOSSARY

**ego** sense of self-esteem or self-importance

**evacuate** remove people from a dangerous place

**geologist** scientist who studies Earth's layers of soil and rock

**lava** hot, liquid rock that pours out of a volcano when it erupts

**magma** melted rock found beneath Earth's surface

**mega-eruption** large volcanic blast, capable of destroying most life on Earth

**molten** melted by heat

**motivation** reason to behave in a certain way

**parole** early release of a prisoner on the promise of good behaviour

**summit** highest point of a hill or mountain

**tundra** cold area where there are no trees and the soil under the ground is permanently frozen

# DISCUSSION QUESTIONS

1. Captain Cold is the Flash's arch-enemy. Why do you think the super hero chose to trust this villain? Did he make the right choice?

2. Do you think Captain Cold's punishment fits his crime? If so, why? If not, how would you have punished the super-villain differently?

3. Using his super-speed, Flash can dash around the world in a split second. If you had super-speed, where in the world would you go? Why?

# WRITING PROMPTS

1. Would you rather have the Flash's super-speed or Captain Cold's powerful cold guns? Write about the power you would choose and why.

2. Write another story where the Flash takes on Captain Cold. Where will they battle next time? Who will win? The choice is up to you.

3. Create your own super hero. First, write about your hero's abilities and powers. Will your hero have super-speed? Can he or she fly? Afterwards, draw a picture of your crime fighter.

# MORE NEW

## ADVENTURES!

WRATH OF THE
WEATHER WIZARD

ATTACK OF
PROFESSOR ZOOM!

SHADOW OF THE SUN

SHELL SHOCKER

GORILLA WARFARE